Zara's Big Messy Day
(That Turned Out Okay)

STORY BY REBEKAH BORUCKI ART BY DANIELLE PIOLI

Rebekah "Bex" Borucki, founder of BEXLIFE® and the BLISSED IN® wellness movement, is a mother of five, best-selling author, meditation and yoga guide, and birth doula. Her mission is to make mental health support and stress management tools accessible to all. Rebekah lives with her family and a barn-full of rescued farm animals on their 8-acre homestead in rural New Jersey.

Danielle Pioli is a multi-passionate independent artist from Brazil. She specializes in children's book illustrations, character design, comic strips, art zines, and more. Danielle is also a hypnotherapist, focused on working with creative people to reach their full artistic potential. Her mission is to spark inspiration through her art, illustrations, comics, zines, poems, songs, and whatever she feels drawn towards.

Illustrated by Danielle Pioli
Content consulting by Nic Strack
Edited by Esther Goldenberg
Author photo by Justin Borucki; Illustrator photo courtesy of Danielle Pioli
Special thanks to Megan Conway Lapp (www.craftyintentions.net) for creating the inspiration for Zara's friend, Worry the Dragon, and to Andi Simmons for bringing him to life

First edition December 2019 — Published by Wheat Penny Press — Printed in Canada
ISBN: 978-1-7340901-0-9; electronic book ISBN: 978-1-7340901-1-6

Fonts used in the design of this book: Oscar Bravo, New Beginnings, and Sofia Pro Soft
The artwork was created digitally, using Adobe Photoshop and pen display by Wacom MobileStudio Pro

DEDICATED TO MRS. MEGAN CASTRO AND HER 2018-2019 SECOND GRADE CLASS AT DR. GERALD H. WOEHR ELEMENTARY SCHOOL. THANK YOU FOR BEING ZARA'S FIRST AUDIENCE.

AND THANK YOU TO OUR "FRIENDS OF ZARA" KICKSTARTER VILLAGE

ALICE GORDON — AMELIE AND JOHN O'HARA — ANDI SIMMONS — ANDREA OWEN — ANITA GOA — ASHA FROST — ATLAS SANCHEZ — AURORA AND BERKELEY LEFFELMAN — AYDEN ALEXANDER — BEA, BEN, KLARA, AND KRISTIAN BUCKLEY — BIG CITY STEVE — BLUMES TRACY — BRAINCURVES (FOR MY THEN, NOW, AND ALWAYS TEACHERS) — CARYN KALI — CHIDIMMA OZOR — CRISTIE RITZ-KING — DANA, KATIE, AND TONY GARCIA — DANIELLE LISS — DAVID AND MARY LYNN PARISE — ELLIE BURROWS GLUCK — ELOISE RUTH AULD — EMMA JEANNE KIRAYOGLU — HARRISON MALONEY — HAYES RYAN BROOKS — IN HONOR OF CATRICE M. JACKSON — IN HONOR OF HARPER AND AUDREY OLSEN — JACQUELINE CARLY — JAIDEN HSU — JAMES AND CURRAN YOUNT — JAXON ANSIS — JODY VALLEE SMITH — KATHRYN — KIM RAYBOULD — LEAH PETERSON — LEESA & MORGAYNE RENÉE — LIANA CISSELL KRESS — MADELEINE C. — MADISON, KAMRYN, ALICE, AND PENELOPE DIPILLA — MELINDA SCIME — NADIA HOLCOMB — NANCY TORRES — ROBBY WERNER — SAGE V. — SAPPHIRE AMIYA GREEN BROOKER — SARAH MCKAY — SHARYN HOLMES — TAKISHA A. — TANYA GEISLER — TAYLOR BUCK — THE MCHENRY FAMILY — TRACY MURPHY — TRINA — VANESSA CHEATWOOD

It was Monday morning, and Mama was busy.

Busy making breakfast.

Busy trying to get Zara's little brother, Sam, to eat breakfast.

Busy getting ready for work.

This is what every morning is like, Zara thought.

Zara never made trouble.

She was in the second grade and had a lot of important jobs and responsibilities.

She always remembered to put her pajamas away, get dressed, and brush her teeth on her own.

Zara even put the cap back on the toothpaste when she was done.

Sam, on the other hand, was always causing a commotion.

PEW
PEW

Zara did her best to pay him no attention, but ignoring Sam was hard.

Sam crashed into Zara with his toy robot, and her orange juice spilled and splattered all over her school clothes.

"Stop it! Stop it! Stop it!"

Zara yelled as she ran to her bedroom and slammed the door.

"Zara," Mama said softly. "You seem upset. I think I know how you feel. I used to stuff so many of my feelings down inside that it felt like I might explode. Grandma taught me something when I was a little girl that helped me a lot. Maybe it can help you, too."

"Next time you start to feel mad or sad or like your feelings are too big to handle, close your eyes. And with a big breath in, pretend there's a bunch of flowers under your nose. Then, blow that big breath out, and pretend you're blowing out candles—like on a birthday cake!"

Zara loved pretending...

Close your eyes, Zara said to herself.

Smell the flowers. She took a deep breath in.

Blow out the candles. She blew that big breath out.

When Zara opened her eyes, she could still hear Sam running around the kitchen, and her clothes were still a mess. But to her surprise, she felt a little better.

PEW

At recess, Penelope laughed at Zara's new light-up shoes.

HAHAHAHAHA

They were a gift from Daddy, and that made them extra special.

But Penelope didn't know that. Or care.

"Hey, everybody, look! Zara's wearing baby shoes! Goo-goo, gaga!"

Zara clenched her hands into fists and twisted her mouth into a grimace. She wanted to yell at Penelope.

But then Zara remembered. She remembered the orange juice. She remembered Mama's words.

And she remembered feeling better.

smell the flowers

blow out the candles

When Zara opened her eyes, Penelope wasn't there. And Zara felt better, not mad or sad at all.

Mama's words worked again!

Zara knew to tell her teacher what happened. Miss Tapper thanked her and promised to help. Zara felt relieved.

Sam likes Chinese food, so Mama didn't spend all of dinnertime reminding him to stay in his seat. After they ate, Zara cleared the table and filled the dishwasher. She enjoyed helping.

Instead of helping Zara,
Sam made a mess with his blocks.

And when Zara tried to build a tower,
Sam sent it tumbling to the floor before
she was done.

Zara wanted to throw a block at him,
but that would only make things worse.

She remembered Mama's words.

When Zara opened her eyes, Sam was still stomping around and making a mess, but she didn't want to throw blocks at him anymore.

"Mama, can you ask Sam to leave my tower alone?" Zara asked.

Mama pretended the blocks were cars and zoomed them back and forth with Sam. Zara built a tower so tall that she had to stand on tippy-toes to put the last block on top.

Mama was busy, but she was never too busy to tuck Zara into bed.

Zara told Mama about her day. She reminded her about the orange juice, and she told her about Penelope teasing her at school. Zara told Mama how mad she got when Sam knocked over her tower, and about all the times she smelled the flowers and blew out the candles.

"Wow!" exclaimed Mama. "It sounds like you had a big day. How do you feel?"

"I didn't like how I felt when I got mad at Sam or when Penelope teased me," Zara replied. "But smelling the flowers and blowing out the candles helped a lot."

"That's wonderful," Mama said with a smile. "All of those feelings are normal. And it's also okay to want to feel better if you're feeling upset. Now you know how to help yourself feel better on your own. Would you like a hug?"

Zara grinned from ear to ear and threw her arms around Mama.

Zara's BIG messy day turned out even BETTER than okay.

A NOTE FOR PARENTS, CAREGIVERS, AND EDUCATORS

My sincere hope is that you and your child(ren) use this story and the practice it offers to create tiny moments of peace throughout your day.

Now that you've read the story with your little one(s), it's time to help them make Zara's practice their own. You're about to play the part of a meditation teacher, but don't worry if you don't have much, or any, experience. Helping a child learn to meditate is easy when you approach the task without any attachment to a perfect outcome.

For a lot of people, meditation means sitting still and thinking about nothing. In 25 years of daily practice, that's never been my goal. My personal definition of meditation is simply taking the time to say to myself, "Yes, I see you. I recognize that you're a thinking, feeling person, and I'm here to listen." That's it! Meditation is taking the time to check in with your feelings and create a little oasis of peace and calm in your day. There are as many effective ways to meditate as there are people on the planet. There's no wrong way to practice. If you can breathe, you can meditate.

The word "relative" will be your new best friend during this process. Instead of finding a perfectly quiet spot for their practice, know that relative quiet will do. It might be too much to expect a child to be perfectly still, but relative stillness (read: not running around in circles) will work just fine. Fidgeting a bit in their seat during meditation is normal—for adults, too. It's of no matter whether you have 2 minutes or 20 to guide their practice. Just taking a few moments to pause can create a total shift in mood and mindset.

Get playful and creative. Using a real candle isn't recommended, so try playing pretend with flowers (real or imitation) and battery-operated tea light candles (you can find fun, color-change versions in craft stores and online). Or, they can use only their imagination like Zara. To help support their practice further, you can download a free PDF coloring page and access a guided meditation video at BexLife.com/zara-bonus.

This simple, three-step practice (close your eyes, inhale, exhale) is meant to create a gentle pause and an opportunity for your child to move their attention from what's bothering or worrying them to something safe and comforting. Over time, you might want to experiment with replacing the flowers and candles with other objects. Let the child guide the process. Soon, they'll have a meditation practice that belongs to only them and a way to access calm and quiet no matter what outside circumstances may be. And that can offer space for more in-depth conversations about their feelings and discussions about peaceful conflict resolution.

Your feedback means the world to me, so please feel encouraged to contact me via my website, BexLife.com, or on Facebook and Instagram @BexLife.

HAPPY MEDITATING!

More "Big Messy" Stories for You

ZARA'S BIG MESSY BEDTIME

ZARA'S BIG MESSY PLAYDATE (PENELOPE RETURNS!)

ZARA'S BIG MESSY GOODBYE

www.WheatPennyPress.com